Clifford's®
SPORTS DAY

Story and pictures by Norman Bridwell

SCHOLASTIC INC.

New York   Toronto   London   Auckland   Sydney
Mexico City   New Delhi   Hong Kong   Buenos Aires

For Jennifer Naomi Morris

© 2003 Scholastic Inc.
90 Old Sherman Turnpike, Danbury, Connecticut 06816

ISBN 0-439-63472-5

Printed in the U.S.A.

Visit scholastic.com for information about our books and authors online!

I'm Emily Elizabeth. My dog is Clifford.

Last week I took him to school for our outdoor Sports Day.

Clifford had never gone to a Sports Day before.

The gym teachers had planned a day
full of races and games.

First was a sack race. Clifford wanted to try it.
The coach said that all his feet had to be in one bag.

I found a sack that was big enough.

Then we were off!

Clifford got an A for effort.

Next came the three-legged race.

Clifford did better at that,
but the race was a little rough on me.

Clifford saw some kids jumping over hurdles.
It looked like fun.

Clifford took a running start. . . .

He tried to jump all the hurdles at once!

CRASH! Jumping hurdles wasn't as easy as he thought.

The next event was tumbling.

Clifford was good at that.

He got a perfect 10.

Afterwards we had a tug-of-war.

Clifford saw that my side was in trouble.

He helped us out.

The other kids didn't like that.
They complained to the coach.

The coach said Clifford couldn't play anymore.

Our Sports Day was almost over by now.
The last event was a softball game.
Clifford stayed to watch.

I knew he wanted to help our team,

but he obeyed the coach.

Even when the other team got a tremendous hit. . .

Clifford didn't try to catch the ball.

But he did catch the ball catcher,
just in time.

He didn't help us win the game...

...but he was the hero of our Sports Day.
Good work, Clifford!